Louisa May

Mountain-Laurel and ...air

Louisa May Alcott

Mountain-Laurel and Maidenhair

1st Edition | ISBN: 978-3-73407-710-4

Place of Publication: Frankfurt am Main, Germany

Year of Publication: 2019

Outlook Verlag GmbH, Germany.

Reproduction of the original.

MOUNTAIN-LAUREL
AND
MAIDENHAIR
BY
LOUISA M. ALCOTT

AUTHOR OF "LITTLE MEN," "LITTLE WOMEN," "MAY FLOWERS," "POPPIES AND WHEAT," ETC.

Illustrated

BOSTON
LITTLE, BROWN, AND COMPANY

University Press
JOHN WILSON AND SON, CAMBRIDGE, U.S.A.

MOUNTAIN-LAUREL AND
MAIDENHAIR

"Here's your breakfast, miss. I hope it's right. Your mother showed me how to fix it, and said I'd find a cup up here."

"Take that blue one. I have not much appetite, and can't eat if things are not nice and pretty. I like the flowers. I've been longing for some ever since I saw them last night."

The first speaker was a red-haired, freckled-faced girl, in a brown calico dress and white apron, with a tray in her hands and an air of timid hospitality in her manner; the second a pale, pretty creature, in a white wrapper and blue net, sitting in a large chair, looking about her with the languid interest of an invalid in a new place. Her eyes brightened as they fell upon a glass of rosy laurel and delicate maidenhair fern that stood among the toast and eggs, strawberries and cream, on the tray.

"Our laurel is jest in blow, and I'm real glad you come in time to see it. I'll bring you a lot, as soon's ever I get time to go for it."

As she spoke, the plain girl replaced the ugly crockery cup and saucer with the pretty china ones pointed out to her, arranged the dishes, and waited to see if anything else was needed.

"What is your name, please?" asked the pretty girl, refreshing herself with a draught of new milk.

"Rebecca. Mother thought I'd better wait on you; the little girls are so noisy and apt to forget. Wouldn't you like a piller to your back? you look so kind of feeble seems as if you wanted to be propped up a mite."

There was so much compassion and good-will in the face and voice, that Emily accepted the offer, and let Rebecca arrange a cushion behind her; then, while the one ate daintily, and the other stirred about an inner room, the talk went on,—for two girls are seldom long silent when together.

"I think the air is going to suit me, for I slept all night and never woke till Mamma had been up ever so long and got things all nicely settled," said Emily, graciously, when the fresh strawberries had been enjoyed, and the bread and butter began to vanish.

"I'm real glad you like it: most folks do, if they don't mind it being plain and quiet up here. It's gayer down at the hotel, but the air ain't half so good, and delicate folks generally like our old place best," answered Becky, as she tossed over a mattress and shook out the sheets with a brisk, capable air pleasant to see.

"I wanted to go to the hotel, but the doctor said it would be too noisy for me, so Mamma was glad to find rooms here. I didn't think a farm-house *could* be so pleasant. That view is perfectly splendid!" and Emily sat up to gaze delightedly out of the window, below which spread the wide intervale, through which the river ran with hay-fields on either side, while along the green slopes of the hills lay farm-houses with garden plots, and big barns waiting for the harvest; and beyond, the rocky, wooded pastures dotted with cattle and musical with cow-bells, brooks, and birds.

A balmy wind kissed a little color into the pale cheeks, the listless eyes brightened as they looked, and the fretful lines vanished from lips that smiled involuntarily at the sweet welcome Nature gave the city child come to rest and play and grow gay and rosy in her green lap.

Becky watched her with interest, and was glad to see how soon the new-comer felt the charm of the place, for the girl loved her mountain home, and thought the old farm-house the loveliest spot in the world.

"When you get stronger I can show you lots of nice views round here. There's a woodsy place behind the house that's just lovely. Down by the laurel bushes is *my* favorite spot, and among the rocks is a cave where I keep things handy when I get a resting-spell now and then, and want to be quiet. Can't get much at home, when there's boarders and five children round in vacation time."

Becky laughed as she spoke, and there was a sweet motherly look in her plain face, as she glanced at the three little red heads bobbing about the door-yard below, where hens cackled, a pet lamb fed, and the old white dog lay blinking in the sun.

"I like children; we have none at home, and Mamma makes such a baby of me I'm almost ashamed sometimes. I want her to have a good rest now, for she has taken care of me all winter and needs it. You shall be my nurse, if I need one; but I hope to be so well soon that I can see to myself. It's so tiresome to be ill!" and Emily sighed as she leaned back among her pillows, with a glance at the little glass which showed her a thin face and shorn head.

"It must be! I never was sick, but I have taken care of sick folks, and have a sight of sympathy for 'em. Mother says I make a pretty good nurse, being strong and quiet," answered Becky, plumping up pillows and folding towels with a gentle despatch which was very grateful to the invalid, who had dreaded a noisy, awkward serving-maid.

"Never ill! how nice that must be! I'm always having colds and headaches, and fusses of some kind. What do you do to keep well, Rebecca?" asked Emily, watching her with interest, as she came in to remove the tray.

"Nothing but work; I haven't time to be sick, and when I'm tuckered out, I go and rest over yonder. Then I'm all right, and buckle to again, as smart as ever;" and every freckle in Becky's rosy face seemed to shine with cheerful strength and courage.

"I'm 'tuckered out' doing nothing," said Emily, amused with the new expression, and eager to try a remedy which showed such fine results in this case. "I shall visit your pet places and do a little work as soon as I am able, and see if it won't set me up. Now I can only dawdle, doze, and read a little. Will you please put those books here on the table? I shall want them by-and-by."

Emily pointed to a pile of blue and gold volumes lying on a trunk, and Becky dusted her hands as she took them up with an air of reverence, for she read on the backs of the volumes names which made her eyes sparkle.

"Do you care for poetry?" asked Emily, surprised at the girl's look and manner.

"Guess I do! don't get much except the pieces I cut out of papers, but I love 'em, and stick 'em in an old ledger, and keep it down in my cubby among the rocks. I do love *that* man's pieces. They seem to go right to the spot somehow;" and Becky smiled at the name of Whittier as if the sweetest of our poets was a dear old friend of hers.

"I like Tennyson better. Do you know him?" asked Emily, with a superior air, for the idea of this farmer's daughter knowing anything about poetry amused her.

"Oh yes, I've got a number of his pieces in my book, and I'm fond of 'em. But this man makes things so kind of true and natural I feel at home with *him*. And this one I've longed to read, though I guess I can't understand much of it. His 'Bumble Bee' was just lovely; with the grass and columbines and the yellow breeches of the bee. I'm never tired of that;" and Becky's face woke up into something like beauty as she glanced hungrily at the Emerson while she dusted the delicate cover that hid the treasures she coveted.

"I don't care much for him, but Mamma does. I like romantic poems, and ballads, and songs; don't like descriptions of clouds, and fields, and bees, and farmers," said Emily, showing plainly that even Emerson's simplest poems were far above her comprehension as yet, because she loved sentiment more than Nature.

"I do, because I know 'em better than love and the romantic stuff most poetry tells about. But I don't pretend to judge, I'm glad of anything I can get. Now if you don't want me I'll pick up my dishes and go to work."

With that Becky went away, leaving Emily to rest and dream with her eyes on the landscape which was giving her better poetry than any her books held. She told her mother about the odd girl, and was sure she would be amusing if she did not forget her place and try to be friends.

"She is a good creature, my dear, her mother's main stay, and works beyond her strength, I am sure. Be kind to the poor girl, and put a little pleasure into her life if you can," answered Mrs. Spenser, as she moved about, settling comforts and luxuries for her invalid.

"I shall *have* to talk to her, as there is no other person of my age in the house. How are the school marms? shall you get on with them, Mamma? It will be so lonely here for us both, if we don't make friends with some one."

"Most intelligent and amiable women all three, and we shall have pleasant times together, I am sure. You may safely cultivate Becky; Mrs. Taylor told me she was a remarkably bright girl, though she may not look it."

"Well, I'll see. But I do hate freckles and big red hands, and round shoulders. She can't help it, I suppose, but ugly things fret me."

"Remember that she has no time to be pretty, and be glad she is so neat and willing. Shall we read, dear? I'm ready now."

Emily consented, and listened for an hour or two while the pleasant voice beside her conjured away all her vapors with some of Mrs. Ewing's charming tales.

"The grass is dry now, and I want to stroll on that green lawn before lunch. You rest, Mamma dear, and let me make discoveries all alone," proposed Emily, when the sun shone warmly, and the instinct of all young creatures for air and motion called her out.

So, with her hat and wrap, and book and parasol, she set forth to explore the new land in which she found herself.

Down the wide, creaking stairs and out upon the door-stone she went, pausing there for a moment to decide where first to go. The sound of some one singing in the rear of the house led her in that direction, and turning the corner she made her first pleasant discovery. A hill rose steeply behind the farm-house, and leaning from the bank was an old apple-tree, shading a spring that trickled out from the rocks and dropped into a mossy trough below. Up the tree had grown a wild grape-vine, making a green canopy over the great log which served as a seat, and some one had planted maidenhair ferns about both seat and spring to flourish beautifully in the damp, shady spot.

"Oh, how pretty! I'll go and sit there. It looks clean, and I can see what is going on in that big kitchen, and hear the singing. I suppose it's Becky's little sisters by the racket."

Emily established herself on the lichen-covered log with her feet upon a stone, and sat enjoying the musical tinkle of the water, with her eyes on the delicate ferns stirring in the wind, and the lively jingle of the multiplication-table chanted by childish voices in her ear.

Presently two little girls with a great pan of beans came to do their work on the back door-step, a third was seen washing dishes at a window, and Becky's brown-spotted gown flew about the kitchen as if a very energetic girl wore it. A woman's voice was heard giving directions, as the speaker was evidently picking chickens somewhere out of sight.

A little of the talk reached Emily and both amused and annoyed her, for it proved that the country people were not as stupid as they looked.

"Oh, well, we mustn't mind if she *is* notional and kind of wearing; she's been sick, and it will take time to get rid of her fretty ways. Jest be pleasant, and take no notice, and that nice mother of hers will make it all right," said the woman's voice.

"How anybody with every mortal thing to be happy with *can* be out-of-sorts passes me. She fussed about every piller, chair, trunk, and mite of food last night, and kept that poor tired lady trotting till I was provoked. She's right pleasant this morning though, and as pretty as a picture in her ruffled gown and that blue thing on her head," answered Becky from the pantry, as she rattled out the pie-board, little dreaming who sat hidden behind the grape-vine festoons that veiled the corner by the spring.

"Well, she's got redder hair 'n' we have, so she needn't be so grand and try to hide it with blue nets," added one little voice.

"Yes, and it's ever so much shorter 'n' ours, and curls all over her head like Daisy's wool. I should think such a big girl would feel real ashamed without no braids," said the other child, proudly surveying the tawny mane that hung over her shoulders,—for like most red-haired people all the children were blessed with luxuriant crops of every shade from golden auburn to regular carrots.

"I think it's lovely. Suppose it had to be cut off when she had the fever. WishI could get rid of my mop, it's such a bother;" and Becky was seen tying a clean towel over the great knot that made her head look very like a copper kettle.

"Now fly round, deary, and get them pies ready. I'll have these fowls on in a minute, and then go to my butter. You run off and see if you can't find some wild strawberries for the poor girl, soon's ever you are through with them beans, children. We must kind of pamper her up for a spell till her appetite comes back," said the mother.

Here the chat ended, and soon the little girls were gone, leaving Becky alone rolling out pie-crust before the pantry window. As she worked her lips moved, and Emily, still peeping through the leaves, wondered what she was saying, for a low murmur rose and fell, emphasized now and then with a thump of the rolling-pin.

"I mean to go and find out. If I stand on that wash-bench I can look in and see her work. I'll show them all that *I'*m *not* 'fussy,' and can be 'right pleasant' if I like."

With this wise resolution Emily went down the little path, and after pausing to examine the churn set out to dry, and the row of pans shining on a neighboring shelf, made her way to the window, mounted the bench while Becky's back was turned, and pushing away the morning-glory vines and scarlet beans that ran up on either side peeped in with such a smiling face that the crossest cook could not have frowned on her as an intruder.

"May I see you work? I can't eat pies, but I like to watch people make them. Do you mind?"

"Not a bit. I'd ask you to come in, but it's dreadful hot here, and not much room," answered Becky, crimping round the pastry before she poured in the custard. "I'm going to make a nice little pudding for you; your mother said you liked 'em; or would you rather have whipped cream with a mite of jelly in it?" asked Becky, anxious to suit her new boarder.

"Whichever is easiest to make. I don't care what I eat. Do tell me what you were saying. It sounded like poetry," said Emily, leaning both elbows on the wide ledge with a pale pink morning-glory kissing her cheek, and a savory odor reaching her nose.

"Oh, I was mumbling some verses. I often do when I work, it sort of helps me along; but it must sound dreadful silly," and Becky blushed as if caught in some serious fault.

"I do it, and it's a great comfort when I lie awake. I should think you *would* want something to help you along, you work so hard. Do you like it, Becky?"

The familiar name, the kind tone, made the plain face brighten with pleasure as its owner said, while she carefully filled a pretty bowl with a golden mixture rich with fresh eggs and country milk,—

7

"No, I don't, but I ought to. Mother isn't as strong as she used to be, and there's a sight to do, and the children to be brought up, and the mortgage to be paid off; so if *I* don't fly round, who will? We are doing real well now, for Mr. Walker manages the farm and gives us our share, so our living is all right; then boarders in summer and my school in winter help a deal, and every year the boys can do more, so I'd be a real sinner to complain if I do have to step lively all day."

Becky smiled as she spoke, and straightened her bent shoulders as if settling her burden for another trudge along the path of duty.

"Do you keep school? Why, how old are you, Becky?" asked Emily, much impressed by this new discovery.

"I'm eighteen. I took the place of a teacher who got sick last fall, and I kept school all winter. Folks seemed to like me, and I'm going to have the same place this year. I'm so glad, for I needn't go away, and the pay is pretty good, as the school is large and the children do well. You can see the school-house down the valley, that red brick one where the roads meet;" and Becky pointed a floury finger, with an air of pride that was pleasant to see.

Emily glanced at the little red house where the sun shone hotly in summer, and all the winds of heaven must rage wildly in winter time, for it stood, as country schools usually do, in the barest, most uninviting spot for miles around.

"Isn't it awful down there in winter?" she asked, with a shiver at the idea of spending days shut up in that forlorn place, with a crowd of rough country children.

"Pretty cold, but we have plenty of wood, and we are used to snow and gales up here. We often coast down, the whole lot of us, and that is great fun. We take our dinners and have games noon-spells, and so we get on first rate; some of my boys are big fellows, older than I am, and they clear the roads and make the fire and look after us, and we are real happy together."

Emily found it so impossible to imagine happiness under such circumstances that she changed the subject by asking in a tone which had unconsciously grown more respectful since this last revelation of Becky's abilities,—

"If you do so well here, why don't you try for a larger school in a better place?"

"Oh, I couldn't leave mother yet; I hope to some day, when the girls are older, and the boys able to get on alone. But I can't go now, for there's a sight of things to do, and mother is always laid up with rheumatism in cold weather. So much butter-making down cellar is bad for her; but she won't let me do that in summer, so I take care of her in winter. I can see to things night and morning, and through the day she's quiet, and sits piecing carpet-rags and resting up for next spring. We made and wove all the carpets in the house, except the parlor one. Mrs. Taylor gave us that, and the curtains, and the easy-chair. Mother takes a sight of comfort in that."

"Mrs. Taylor is the lady who first came to board here, and told us and others about it," said Emily.

"Yes, and she's the kindest lady in the world! I'll tell you all about her some day, it's real interesting; now I must see to my pies, and get the vegetables on," answered Becky, glancing at the gay clock in the kitchen with an anxious look.

"Then I won't waste any more of your precious time. May I sit in that pretty place; or is it your private bower?" asked Emily, as she dismounted from the wash-bench.

"Yes, indeed you may. That's mother's resting place when work is done. Father made the spring long ago, and I put the ferns there. She can't go rambling round, and she likes pretty things, so we fixed it up for her, and she takes comfort there nights."

Becky bustled off to the oven with her pies, and Emily roamed away to the big barn to lie on the hay, enjoying the view down the valley, as she thought over what she had seen and heard, and very naturally contrasted her own luxurious and tenderly guarded life with this other girl's, so hard and dull and narrow. Working all summer and teaching all winter in that dismal little school-house, with no change but home cares and carpet-weaving! It looked horrible to pleasure-loving Emily, who led the happy, care-free life of girls of her class, with pleasures of all sorts, and a future of still greater luxury, variety, and happiness, opening brightly before her.

It worried her to think of any one being contented with such a meagre share of the good things of life, when she was unsatisfied in spite of the rich store showered upon her. She could not understand it, and fell asleep wishing every one could be comfortable,—it was so annoying to see them grubbing in kitchens, teaching in bleak school-houses among snow-drifts, and wearing ugly calico gowns.

A week or two of quiet, country fare and the bracing mountain air worked wonders for the invalid, and every one rejoiced to see the pale cheeks begin to grow round and rosy, the languid eyes to brighten, and the feeble girl who used to lie on her sofa half the day now go walking about with her alpenstock, eager to explore all the pretty nooks among the hills. Her mother blessed Mrs. Taylor for suggesting this wholesome place. The tired "school marms," as

Emily called the three young women who were their fellow-boarders, congratulated her as well as themselves on the daily improvement in strength and spirits all felt; and Becky exulted in the marvellous effects of her native air, aided by mother's good cookery and the cheerful society of the children, whom the good girl considered the most remarkable and lovable youngsters in the world.

Emily felt like the queen of this little kingdom, and was regarded as such by every one, for with returning health she lost her fretful ways, and, living with simple people, soon forgot her girlish airs and vanities, becoming very sweet and friendly with all about her. The children considered her a sort of good fairy who could grant wishes with magical skill, as various gifts plainly proved. The boys were her devoted servants, ready to run errands, "hitch up" and take her to drive at any hour, or listen in mute delight when she sang to her guitar in the summer twilight.

But to Becky she was a special godsend and comfort, for before the first month had gone they were good friends, and Emily had made a discovery which filled her head with brilliant plans for Becky's future, in spite of her mother's warnings, and the sensible girl's own reluctance to be dazzled by enthusiastic prophecies and dreams.

It came about in this way. Some three weeks after the two girls met, Emily went one evening to their favorite trysting-place,—Becky's bower among the laurels. It was a pretty nook in the shadow of a great gray bowlder near the head of the green valley which ran down to spread into the wide intervale below. A brook went babbling among the stones and grass and sweet-ferns, while all the slope was rosy with laurel-flowers in their time, as the sturdy bushes grew thickly on the hill-side, down the valley, and among the woods that made a rich background for these pink and white bouquets arranged with Nature's own careless grace.

Emily liked this spot, and ever since she had been strong enough to reach it, loved to climb up and sit there with book and work, enjoying the lovely panorama before her. Floating mists often gave her a constant succession of pretty pictures; now a sunny glimpse of the distant lake, then the church spire peeping above the hill, or a flock of sheep feeding in the meadow, a gay procession of young pilgrims winding up the mountain, or a black cloud heavy with a coming storm, welcome because of the glorious rainbow and its shadow which would close the pageant.

Unconsciously the girl grew to feel not only the beauty but the value of these quiet hours, to find a new peace, refreshment, and happiness, bubbling up in her heart as naturally as the brook gushed out among the mossy rocks, and went singing away through hay-fields and gardens, and by dusty roads, till it met the river and rolled on to the sea. Something dimly stirred in her, and the healing spirit that haunts such spots did its sweet ministering till the innocent soul began to see that life was not perfect without labor as well as love, duty as well as happiness, and that true contentment came from within, not from without.

On the evening we speak of, she went to wait for Becky, who would join her as soon as the after-supper chores were done. In the little cave which held a few books, a dipper, and a birch-bark basket for berries, Emily kept a sketching block and a box of pencils, and often amused herself by trying to catch some of the lovely scenes before her. These efforts usually ended in a humbler attempt, and a good study of an oak-tree, a bit of rock, or a clump of ferns was the result. This evening the sunset was so beautiful she could not draw, and remembering that somewhere in Becky's scrap-book there was a fine description of such an hour by some poet, she pulled out the shabby old volume, and began to turn over the leaves.

She had never cared to look at it but once, having read all the best of its contents in more attractive volumes, so Becky kept it tucked away in the farther corner of her rustic closet, and evidently thought it a safe place to conceal a certain little secret which Emily now discovered. As she turned the stiff pages filled with all sorts of verses, good, bad, and indifferent, a sheet of paper appeared on which was scribbled these lines in school-girl handwriting:

—

MOUNTAIN-LAUREL

My bonnie flower, with truest joy
    Thy welcome face I see,
The world grows brighter to my eyes,
    And summer comes with thee.
My solitude now finds a friend,
    And after each hard day,
I in my mountain garden walk,
    To rest, or sing, or pray.

All down the rocky slope is spread
    Thy veil of rosy snow,
And in the valley by the brook,
    Thy deeper blossoms grow.
The barren wilderness grows fair,
    Such beauty dost thou give;
And human eyes and Nature's heart
    Rejoice that thou dost live.

Each year I wait thy coming, dear,
 Each year I love thee more,
For life grows hard, and much I need
 Thy honey for my store.
So, like a hungry bee, I sip
 Sweet lessons from thy cup,
And sitting at a flower's feet,
 My soul learns to look up.

No laurels shall I ever win,
 No splendid blossoms bear,
But gratefully receive and use
 God's blessed sun and air;
And, blooming where my lot is cast
 Grow happy and content,
Making some barren spot more fair,
 For a humble life well spent.

"She wrote it herself!"—P<small>AGE</small> **23.**

"She wrote it herself! I can't believe it!" said Emily, as she put down the paper, looking rather startled, for she *did* believe it, and felt as if she had suddenly looked into a fellow-creature's heart. "I thought her just an ordinary girl, and here she is a poet, writing verses that make me want to cry! I don't suppose they *are* very good, but they seem to come right out of her heart, and touch me with the longing and the patience or the piety in them. Well, I *am* surprised!" and Emily read the lines again, seeing the faults more plainly than before, but still feeling that the girl put herself into them, vainly trying to express what the wild flower was to her in the loneliness which comes to those who have a little spark of the divine fire burning in their souls.

"Shall I tell her I've found it out? I must! and see if I can't get her verses printed. Of course she has more tucked away somewhere. That is what she hums to herself when she's at work, and won't tell me about when I ask. Sly thing! to be so bashful and hide her gift. I'll tease her a bit and see what she says. Oh dear, I wish *I* could do it! Perhaps she'll be famous some day, and then I'll have the glory of discovering her."

With that consolation Emily turned over the pages of the ledger and found several more bits of verse, some very good for an untaught girl, others very faulty, but all having a certain strength of feeling and simplicity of language unusual in the effusions of young maidens at the sentimental age.

Emily had a girlish admiration for talent of any kind, and being fond of poetry, was especially pleased to find that her humble friend possessed the power of writing it. Of course she exaggerated Becky's talent, and as she waited for her, felt sure that she had discovered a feminine Burns among the New Hampshire hills, for all the verses were about natural and homely objects, touched into beauty by sweet words or tender sentiment. She had time to build a splendid castle in the air and settle Becky in it with a crown of glory on her head, before the quiet figure in a faded sunbonnet came slowly up the slope with the glow of sunset on a tired but tranquil face.

"Sit here and have a good rest, while I talk to you," said Emily, eager to act the somewhat dramatic scene she had planned. Becky sunk upon the red cushion prepared for her, and sat looking down at the animated speaker, as Emily, perched on a mossy stone before her, began the performance.

"Becky, did you ever hear of the Goodale children? They lived in the country and wrote poetry and grew to be famous."

"Oh yes, I've read their poems and like 'em very much. Do you know 'em?" and Becky looked interested at once.

"No, but I once met a girl who was something like them, only she didn't have such an easy time as they did, with a father to help, and a nice Sky-farm, and good luck generally. I've tried to write verses myself, but I always get into a muddle, and give it up. This makes me interested in other girls who *can* do it, and I want to help my friend. I'm *sure* she has talent, and I'd so like to give her a lift in some way. Let me read you a piece of hers and see what you think of it."

"Do!" and Becky threw off the sunbonnet, folded her hands round her knees, and composed herself to listen with such perfect unconsciousness of what was coming that Emily both laughed at the joke and blushed at the liberty she felt she was taking with the poor girl's carefully hidden secret.

Becky was sure now that Emily was going to read something of her own after this artful introduction, and began to smile as the paper was produced and the first four lines read in a tone that was half timid, half triumphant. Then with a cry she seized and crumpled up the paper, exclaiming almost fiercely,—

"It's mine! Where did you get it? How dar'st you touch it?"

Emily fell upon her knees with a face and voice so full of penitence, pleasure, sympathy, and satisfaction, that Becky's wrath was appeased before her friend's explanation ended with these soothing and delightful words,—

"That's all, dear, and I beg your pardon. But I'm sure you will be famous if you keep on, and I shall yet see a volume of poems by Rebecca Moore of Rocky Nook, New Hampshire."

Becky hid her face as if shame, surprise, wonder, and joy filled her heart too full and made a few happy tears drop on the hands so worn with hard work, when they ached to be holding a pen and trying to record the fancies that sung in her brain as ceaselessly as the soft sough of the pines or the ripple of the brook murmured in her ear when she sat here alone. She could not express the vague longings that stirred in her soul; she could only feel and dimly strive to understand and utter them, with no thought of fame or fortune,—for she was a humble creature, and never knew that the hardships of her life were pressing out the virtues of her nature as the tread of careless feet crush the sweet perfume from wild herbs.

Presently she looked up, deeply touched by Emily's words and caresses, and her blue eyes shone like stars as her face beamed with something finer than mere beauty, for the secrets of her innocent heart were known to this friend now, and it was very sweet to accept the first draught of confidence and praise.

"I don't mind much, but I was scared for a minute. No one knows but Mother, and she laughs at me, though she don't care if it makes me happy. I'm glad you like my scribbling, but really I never think or hope of being anybody. I couldn't, you know! but it's real nice to have you say I *might* and to make believe for a little while."

"But why not, Becky? The Goodale girls did, and half the poets in the world were poor, ignorant people at first, you know. It only needs time and help, and the gift will grow, and people see it; and then the glory and the money will come," cried Emily, quite carried away by her own enthusiasm and good-will.

"Could I get any money by these things?" asked Becky, looking at the crumpled paper lying under a laurel-bush.

"Of course you could, dear! Let me have some of them, and I'll show you that I know good poetry when I see it. You will believe if some bank-bills come with the paper the verses appear in, I hope?"

Blind to any harm she might do by exciting vain hopes in her eagerness to cheer and help, Emily made this rash proposal in all good faith, meaning to pay for the verses herself if no editor was found to accept them.

Becky looked half bewildered by this brilliant prospect, and took a long breath, as if some hand had lifted a heavy burden a little way from her weary back, for stronger than ambition for herself was love for her family, and the thought of help for them was sweeter than any dream of fame.

"Yes, I would! oh, if I only *could*, I'd be the happiest girl in the world! But I can't believe it, Emily. I heard Mrs. Taylor say that only the *very best* poetry paid, and mine is poor stuff, I know well enough."

"Of course it needs polishing and practice and all that; but I'm sure it is oceans better than half the sentimental twaddle we see in the papers, and I *know* that some of those pieces *are* paid for, because I have a friend who is in a newspaper office, and he told me so. Yours are quaint and simple and some very original. I'm sure that ballad of the old house is lovely, and I want to send it to Whittier. Mamma knows him; it's the sort he likes, and he is so kind to every one, he will criticise it, and be interested when she tells him about you. Do let me!"

"I never could in the world! It would be so bold, Mother would think I was crazy. I love Mr. Whittier, but I wouldn't dar'st to show him my nonsense, though reading his beautiful poetry helps me ever so much."

Becky looked and spoke as if her breath had been taken away by this audacious proposal; and yet a sudden delicious hope sprung up in her heart that there might, perhaps, be a spark of real virtue in the little fire which burned within her, warming and brightening her dull life.

"Let us ask Mamma; she will tell us what is best to do first, for she knows all sorts of literary people, and won't say any more than you want her to. I'm bent on having my way, Becky, and the more modest you are, the surer I am that you are a genius. Real geniuses always *are* shy; so you just make up your mind to give me the best of your pieces, and let me prove that I'm right."

It was impossible to resist such persuasive words, and Becky soon yielded to the little siren who was luring her out of her safe, small pool into the deeper water that looks so blue and smooth till the venturesome paper boats get into the swift eddies, or run aground upon the rocks and sandbars.

The greatest secrecy was to be preserved, and no one but Mrs. Spenser was to know what a momentous enterprise was afoot. The girls sat absorbed in their brilliant plans till it was nearly dark, then groped their way home hand in hand, leaving another secret for the laurels to keep and dream over through their long sleep, for blossom time was past, and the rosy faces turning pale in the July sun.

Neither of the girls forgot the talk they had that night in Emily's room, for she led her captive straight to her mother, and told her all their plans and aspirations without a moment's delay.

Mrs. Spenser much regretted her daughter's well-meant enthusiasm, but fearing harm might be done, very wisely tried to calm the innocent excitement of both by the quiet matter-of-fact way in which she listened to the explanation Emily gave her, read the verses timidly offered by Becky, and then said, kindly but firmly:—

"This is not poetry, my dear girls, though the lines run smoothly enough, and the sentiment is sweet. It would bring neither fame nor money, and Rebecca puts more real truth, beauty, and poetry into her dutiful daily life than in any lines she has written."

"We had such a lovely plan for Becky to come to town with me, and see the world, and write, and be famous. How can you spoil it all?"

"My foolish little daughter, I must prevent you from spoiling this good girl's life by your rash projects. Becky will see that I am wise, though you do not, and *she* will understand this verse from my favorite poet, and lay it to heart:—

"So near is grandeur to our dust,
So nigh is God to man,
When Duty whispers low, 'Thou must!'
The youth replies, 'I can!'"

"I do! I will! please go on," and Becky's troubled eyes grew clear and steadfast as she took the words home to herself, resolving to live up to them.

"Oh, mother!" cried Emily, thinking her very cruel to nip their budding hopes in this way.

"I know you won't believe it now, nor be able to see all that I mean perhaps, but time will teach you both to own that I am right, and to value the substance more than the shadow," continued Mrs. Spenser. "Many girls write verses and think they are poets; but it is only a passing mood, and fortunately for the world, and for them also, it soon dies out in some more genuine work or passion. Very few have the real gift, and those to whom it *is* given wait and work and slowly reach the height of their powers. Many delude themselves, and try to persuade the world that they can sing; but it is waste of time, and ends in disappointment, as the mass of sentimental rubbish we all see plainly proves. Write your little verses, my dear, when the spirit moves,—it is a harmless pleasure, a real comfort, and a good lesson for you; but do not neglect higher duties or deceive yourself with false hopes and vain dreams. 'First live, then write,' is a good motto for ambitious young people. A still better for us all is, 'Do the duty that lies nearest;' and the faithful performance of that, no matter how humble it is, will be the best help for whatever talent may lie hidden in us, ready to bloom when the time comes. Remember this, and do not let my enthusiastic girl's well-meant but unwise prophecies and plans unsettle you, and unfit you for the noble work you are doing."

"Thank you, ma'am! I *will* remember; I know you are right, and I won't be upset by foolish notions. I never imagined before that I *could* be a poet; but it sounded so sort of splendid, I thought maybe it *might* happen to me, by-and-by, as it does to other folks. I won't lot on it, but settle right down and do my work cheerful."

As she listened, Becky's face had grown pale and serious, even a little sad; but as she answered, her eyes shone, her lips were firm, and her plain face almost beautiful with the courage and confidence that sprung up within her. She saw the wisdom of her friend's advice, felt the kindness of showing her the mistake frankly, and was grateful for it,—conscious in her own strong, loving heart that it *was* better to live and work for others than to dream and strive for herself alone.

Mrs. Spenser was both surprised and touched by the girl's look, words, and manner, and her respect much increased by the courage and good temper with which she saw her lovely castle in the air vanish like smoke, leaving the hard reality looking harder than ever, after this little flight into the fairy regions of romance.

She talked long with the girls, and gave them the counsel all eager young people need, yet are very slow to accept till experience teaches them its worth. As the friend of many successful literary people, Mrs. Spenser was constantly receiving the confidences of unfledged scribblers, each of whom was sure that he or she had something valuable to add to the world's literature. Her advice was always the same, "Work and wait;" and only now and then was a young poet or author found enough in earnest to do both, and thereby prove to themselves and others either that they *did* possess power, or did not, and so settle the question forever. "First live, then write," proved a *quietus* for many, and "Do the duty that lies nearest" satisfied the more sincere that they could be happy without fame. So, thanks to this wise and kindly woman, a large number of worthy youths and maidens ceased dreaming and fell to work, and the world was spared reams of feeble verse and third-rate romances.

After that night Becky spent fewer spare hours in her nest, and more in reading with Emily, who lent her books and helped her to understand them,— both much assisted by Mrs. Spenser, who marked passages, suggested authors, and explained whatever puzzled them. Very happy bits of time were these, and very precious to both, as Emily learned to see and appreciate the humbler, harder side of life, and Becky got delightful glimpses into the beautiful world of art, poetry, and truth, which gave her better food for heart and brain than sentimental musings or blind efforts to satisfy the hunger of her nature with verse-writing.

Their favorite places were in the big barn, on the front porch, or by the spring. This last was Emily's schoolroom, and she both taught and learned many useful lessons there.

One day as Becky came to rest a few minutes and shell peas, Emily put down her book to help; and as the pods flew, she said, nodding toward the delicate ferns that grew thickly all about the trough, the rock, and the grassy bank,—

"We have these in our greenhouse, but I never saw them growing wild before, and I don't find them anywhere up here. How did you get such beauties, and make them do so well?"

"Oh, they grow in nooks on the mountain hidden under the taller ferns, and in sly corners. But they don't grow like these, and die soon unless transplanted and taken good care of. They always make me think of you,—so graceful and delicate, and just fit to live with tea-roses in a hot-house, and go to balls in beautiful ladies' *bo*kays," answered Becky, smiling at her new friend, always so dainty, and still so delicate in spite of the summer's rustication.

"Thank you! I suppose I shall never be very strong or able to do much; so I *am* rather like a fern, and do live in a conservatory all winter, as I can't go out a great deal. An idle thing, Becky!" and Emily sighed, for she was born frail, and even her tenderly guarded life could not give her the vigor of other girls.

But the sigh changed to a smile as she added,—

"If I am like the fern, you are like your own laurel,—strong, rosy, and able to grow anywhere. I want to carry a few roots home, and see if they won't grow in my garden. Then you will have me, and I you. I only hope *your* plant will do as well as mine does here."

"It won't! ever so many folks have taken roots away, but they never thrive in gardens as they do on the hills where they belong. So I tell 'em to leave the dear bushes alone, and come up here and enjoy 'em in their own place. You might keep a plant of it in your hot-house, and it would blow I dare say; but it would never be half so lovely as my acres of them, and I guess it would only make you sad, seeing it so far from home, and pale and pining," answered Becky, with her eyes on the green slopes where the mountain-laurel braved the wintry snow, and came out fresh and early in the spring.

"Then I'll let it alone till I come next summer. But don't you take any of the fern into the house in the cold weather? I should think it would grow in your sunny windows," said Emily, pleased by the fancy that it resembled herself.

"I tried it, but it needs a damp place, and our cold nights kill it. No, it won't grow in our old house; but I cover it with leaves, and the little green sprouts come up as hearty as can be out here. The shade, the spring, the shelter of the rock, keep it alive, you see, so it's no use trying to move it."

Both sat silent for a few minutes, as their hands moved briskly and they thought of their different lots. An inquisitive ray of sunshine peeped in at them, touching Becky's hair till it shone like red gold. The same ray dazzled Emily's eyes; she put up her hand to pull her hat-brim lower, and touched the little curls on her forehead. This recalled her pet grievance, and made her say impatiently, as she pushed the thick short locks under her net,—

"My hair is *such* a plague! I don't know what I am to do when I go into society by-and-by. This crop is so unbecoming, and I can't match my hair anywhere, it is such a peculiar shade of golden-auburn."

"It's a pretty color, and I think the curls much nicer than a boughten switch," said Becky, quite unconscious that her own luxuriant locks were of the true Titian red, and would be much admired by artistic eyes.

"I don't! I shall send to Paris to match it, and then wear a braid round my head as you do sometimes. I suppose it will cost a fortune, but I *won't* have a strong-minded crop. A friend of mine got a lovely golden switch for fifty dollars."

"My patience! do folks pay like that for false hair?" asked Becky, amazed.

"Yes, indeed. White hair costs a hundred, I believe, if it is long. Why, you could get ever so much for yours if you ever wanted to sell it. I'll take part of it, for in a little while mine will be as dark, and I'd like to wear your hair, Becky."

"Don't believe Mother would let me. She is very proud of our red heads. If I ever do cut it, you shall have some. I may be hard up and glad to sell it perhaps. My sakes! I smell the cake burning!" and off flew Becky to forget the chat in her work.

Emily did not forget it, and hoped Becky would be tempted, for she really coveted one of the fine braids, but felt shy about asking the poor girl for even a part of her one beauty.

So July and August passed pleasantly and profitably to both girls, and in September they were to part. No more was said about poetry; and Emily soon became so interested in the busy, practical life about her that her own high-flown dreams were quite forgotten, and she learned to enjoy the sweet prose of daily labor.

One breezy afternoon as she and her mother sat resting from a stroll on the way-side bank among the golden-rod and asters, they saw Becky coming up the long hill with a basket on her arm. She walked slowly, as if lost in thought, yet never missed pushing aside with a decided gesture of her foot every stone that lay in her way. There were many in that rocky path, but Becky left it smoother as she climbed, and paused now and then to send some especially sharp or large one spinning into the grassy ditch beside the road.

"Isn't she a curious girl, Mamma? so tired after her long walk to town, yet so anxious not to leave a stone in the way," said Emily, as they watched her slow approach.

"A very interesting one to me, dear, because under that humble exterior lies a fine, strong character. It is like Becky to clear her way, even up a dusty hill where the first rain will wash out many more stones. Let us ask her why she does it. I've observed the habit before, and always meant to ask," replied Mrs. Spenser.

"Here we are! Come and rest a minute, Becky, and tell us if you mend roads as well as ever so many other things," called Emily, beckoning with a smile, as the girl looked up and saw them.

"Oh, it's a trick of mine; I caught it of Father when I was a little thing, and do it without knowing it half the time," said Becky, sinking down upon a mossy rock, as if rest were welcome.

"Why did he do it?" asked Emily, who knew that her friend loved to talk of her father.

"Well, it's a family failing I guess, for his father did the same, only *he* began with his farm and let the roads alone. The land used to be pretty much all rocks up here, you know, and farmers had to clear the ground if they wanted crops. It was a hard fight, and took a sight of time and patience to grub out roots and blast rocks and pick up stones that seemed to grow faster than anything else. But they kept on, and now see!"

As she spoke, Becky pointed proudly to the wide, smooth fields lying before them, newly shorn of grass or grain, waving with corn, or rich in garden crops ripening for winter stores. Here and there were rocky strips unreclaimed, as if to show what had been done; and massive stone walls surrounded pasture, field, and garden.

"A good lesson in patience and perseverance, my dear, and does great honor to the men who made the wilderness blossom like the rose," said Mrs. Spenser.

"Then you can't wonder that they loved it and we want to keep it. I guess it would break Mother's heart to sell this place, and we are all working as hard as ever we can to pay off the mortgage. Then we'll be just the happiest family in New Hampshire," said Becky, fondly surveying the old farm-house, the rocky hill, and the precious fields won from the forest.

"You never need fear to lose it; we will see to that if you will let us," began Mrs. Spenser, who was both a rich and a generous woman.

"Oh, thank you! but we won't need help I guess; and if we should, Mrs. Taylor made us promise to come to her," cried Becky. "She found us just in our hardest time, and wanted to fix things then; but we are proud in our way, and Mother said she'd rather work it off if she could. Then what did that dear lady do but talk to the folks round here, and show 'em how a branch railroad down to Peeksville would increase the value of the land, and how good this valley would be for strawberries and asparagus and garden truck if we could only get it to market. Some of the rich men took up the plan, and we hope it will be done this fall. It will be the making of us, for our land is first-rate for small crops, and the children can help at that, and with a *deepot* close by it would be such easy work. That's what I call helping folks to help themselves. Won't it be grand?"

Becky looked so enthusiastic that Emily could not remain uninterested, though market-gardening did not sound very romantic.

"I hope it will come, and next year we shall see you all hard at it. What a good woman Mrs. Taylor is!"

"Ain't she? and the sad part of it is, she can't do and enjoy all she wants to, because her health is so poor. She was a country girl, you know, and went to work in the city as waiter in a boarding-house. A rich man fell in love with her and married her, and she took care of him for years, and he left her all his money. She was quite broken down, but she wanted to make his name loved and honored after his death, as he hadn't done any good while he lived; so she gives away heaps, and is never tired of helping poor folks and doing all sorts of grand things to make the world better. I call that splendid!"

"So do I, yet it is only what you are doing in a small way, Becky," said Mrs. Spenser, as the girl paused out of breath. "Mrs. Taylor clears the stones out of people's paths, making their road easier to climb than hers has been, and leaving behind her fruitful fields for others to reap. This is a better work than making verses, for it is the real poetry of life, and brings to those who give themselves to it, no matter in what humble ways, something sweeter than fame and more enduring than fortune."

"So it does! I see that now, and know why we love Father as we do, and want to keep what he worked so hard to give us. He used to say every stone cleared away was just so much help to the boys; and he used to tell me his plans as I trotted after him round the farm, helping all I could, being the oldest, and like him, he said."

Becky paused with full eyes, for not even to these good friends could she ever tell the shifts and struggles in which she had bravely borne her part during the long hard years that had wrested the little homestead from the stony-hearted hills.

The musical chime of a distant clock reminded her that supper time was near, and she sprang up as if much refreshed by this pleasant rest by the way-side. As she pulled out her handkerchief, a little roll of pale blue ribbon fell from her pocket, and Emily caught it up, exclaiming mischievously, "Are you going to make yourself fine next Sunday, when Moses Pennel calls, Becky?"

"Just as they were parting for bed, in rushed one of the boys with the exciting news."—PAGE 45.

The girl laughed and blushed as she said, carefully folding up the ribbon,—

"I'm going to do something with it that I like a sight better than that. Poor Moses won't come any more, I guess. I'm not going to leave Mother till the girls can take my place, and only then to teach, if I can get a good school somewhere near."

"We shall see!" and Emily nodded wisely.

"We shall!" and Becky nodded decidedly, as she trudged on up the steep hill beside Mrs. Spenser, while Emily walked slowly behind, poking every stone she saw into the grass, unmindful of the detriment to her delicate shoes, being absorbed in a new and charming idea of trying to follow Mrs. Taylor's example in a small way.

A week later the last night came, and just as they were parting for bed, in rushed one of the boys with the exciting news that the railroad surveyors were in town, the folks talking about the grand enterprise, and the fortune of the place made forever.

Great was the rejoicing in the old farm-house; the boys cheered, the little girls danced, the two mothers dropped a happy tear as they shook each other's hands, and Emily embraced Becky, tenderly exclaiming,—"There, you dear thing, is a great stone shoved out of *your* way, and a clear road to fortune at last; for I shall tell all my friends to buy your butter and eggs, and fruit and pigs, and everything you send to market on that blessed railroad."

"A keg of our best winter butter is going by stage express to-morrow anyway; and when our apples come, we shan't need a railroad to get 'em to you, my darling dear," answered Becky, holding the delicate girl in her arms with a look and gesture half sisterly, half motherly, wholly fond and grateful.

When Emily got to her room, she found that butter and apples were not all the humble souvenirs offered in return for many comfortable gifts to the whole family.

On the table, in a pretty birch-bark cover, lay several of Becky's best poems neatly copied, as Emily had expressed a wish to keep them; and round the rustic volume, like a ring of red gold, lay a great braid of Becky's hair, tied with the pale blue ribbon she had walked four miles to buy, that her present might look its best.

Of course there were more embraces and kisses, and thanks and loving words, before Emily at last lulled herself to sleep planning a Christmas box, which should supply every wish and want of the entire family if she could find them out.

Next morning they parted; but these were not mere summer friends, and they did not lose sight of one another, though their ways lay far apart. Emily had found a new luxury to bring more pleasure into life, a new medicine to strengthen soul and body; and in helping others, she helped herself wonderfully.

Becky went steadily on her dutiful way, till the homestead was free, the lads able to work the farm alone, the girls old enough to fill her place, and the good mother willing to rest at last among her children. Then Becky gave herself to teaching,—a noble task, for which she was well fitted, and in which she found both profit and pleasure, as she led her flock along the paths from which she removed the stumbling-blocks for their feet, as well as for her own. She put her poetry into her life, and made of it "a grand sweet song" in which beauty and duty rhymed so well that the country girl became a more useful, beloved, and honored woman than if she had tried to sing for fame which never satisfies.

So each symbolical plant stood in its own place, and lived its appointed life. The delicate fern grew in the conservatory among tea-roses and camellias, adding grace to every bouquet of which it formed a part, whether it faded in a ball-room, or was carefully cherished by some poor invalid's bed-side,—a frail thing, yet with tenacious roots and strong stem, nourished by memories of the rocky nook where it had learned its lesson so well. The mountain-laurel clung to the bleak hillside, careless of wintry wind and snow, as its sturdy branches spread year by year, with its evergreen leaves for Christmas cheer, its rosy flowers for spring-time, its fresh beauty free to all as it clothed the wild valley with a charm that made a little poem of the lovely spot where the pines whispered, woodbirds sang, and the hidden brook told the sweet message it brought from the mountain-top where it was born.